FIVE FOR THE TRAIL

Mark L. Redmond

Although the cowboy's side-arm was commonly called a six-shooter, a careful cowboy only loaded five chambers most of the time. By leaving an empty chamber under the hammer, he eliminated the risk of shooting himself or his horse if his gun was bumped, dropped, or snagged by the brush through which he was riding. The title for this collection of short stories comes from that old West safety measure. When a cowboy sensed or saw trouble coming, he thumbed a cartridge into the empty chamber and faced the situation with his six-shooter fully loaded. With that practice in mind, I "thumbed" a sixth story into this collection—just for fun. I hope you enjoy all six stories.

M.L.R.

Contents

CRAWL OFF and DIE

Bailey O'Toole sat leaning against a boulder and watched his back trail. Sweat trickled down both cheeks and dripped from his stubble-covered chin onto his damp shirt. A fly buzzed around his head several times before landing on the brim of Bailey's Stetson, but he seemed not to notice. His full attention was focused on the trail he had followed to the top of the butte. He swore softly when he spotted the small cloud of dust half a mile from its base. Whoever was after him was not only good at reading sign but also tenacious on a trail.

Closing his eyes, Bailey lifted his work-hardened hands to his face and pressed his fingertips against his eyelids. The excruciating pain lessened ever so slightly for a moment, and he tried desperately to focus his thoughts on the events of the past six months. Six months earlier, Bailey had been enjoying what he had believed to be the best life possible. He had sat at the table, celebrating his twentieth birthday with the three people he loved most. At the close of the meal, Bailey's father had struggled to stand behind his chair.

He had smiled across the table, swallowed hard, and then spoken.

"Son, there's not a prouder father in all of Tucson—or for that matter, in all of Arizona—than me. I know that folks tend to brag on me for coming home from the war minus a leg and then starting the mercantile. But that was nothing. I started the mercantile because your ma and I couldn't think of much else I was good for. Then when the cholera took your ma and your sister twelve years ago—"

Bailey's father had stopped to wipe his eyes with a thumb and forefinger before continuing.

"Well, you and me kept working that mercantile, which was already doing pretty well. Folks bragged on me for not quitting then, too, but that was nothing. What folks didn't know is that I had one of the finest young assistants on God's earth working for me. What folks didn't know is that my little Bailey didn't just work himself half to death during the daytime; he—" his father had stopped and wiped his eyes again. He had waited a moment to regain his composure. Bailey had looked at his father and had been surprised to see that although his father was smiling, there were tears in his eyes. He had continued in a softer tone.

"He also helped to heal his pa's heart and give him a reason to open the mercantile each morning." Bailey's father had taken a deep breath and then had reached into the inside pocket of his vest to pull out a folded paper.

"As a result, I now own the most successful dry goods mercantile in Tucson. Allow me to correct myself. *We* now own the most successful mercantile in Tucson, Pardner."

Still smiling, Bailey's father had handed him the paper that declared him half owner of his father's mercantile.

Bailey pulled his hands from his sweaty face and shook his head slightly. Shading his eyes with both hands, he looked again at his back trail. When his eyes finally focused, he could see that the cloud of dust was still moving toward him. Muttering a curse, Bailey dragged himself into the saddle. As he started down the back side of the butte, he pulled his hat brim down as far as possible to shield his eyes from the sun. Bailey closed his eyes and let his horse find its own way through the scattered rocks that covered the side of the butte. With each step his horse took, he felt as if someone had pounded his head with a fence post. Occasionally he took a sip of water from his canteen, but his stomach was too sick for him to risk swallowing anything else. Past experiences with his headaches had taught him that whatever he ate wouldn't stay down anyway.

"Congratulations, Bailey," Doc Atwood had said as he had left to tend to a patient that night after supper.

"Did you know about this partnership idea?" Bailey had asked.

Doc had smiled, shaking Bailey's hand and patting him on the shoulder. "Your father never breathed a word about it to me. I found out when you did. I reckon he knew you'd see me grinning and get suspicious. I couldn't agree with him more, though."

Then Doc's expression had grown serious. "I've written to an old friend in Boston about your headaches. I expect an answer from him in a week or so. In the meantime, use the medicine I gave you when you need to."

That was the last time Bailey had seen the man who had been his father's best friend and Bailey's "Uncle Bill" as he had been growing up. A week later, three nameless drifters had decided to rob the bank in Tucson while Bailey's pa and Doc Atwood had been in there on business.

When a teller had pulled a gun from beneath the counter, the drifters had started shooting at everyone. Neither Doc nor Bailey's pa had been carrying a gun, but both had been killed along with the foolish teller, one other customer, and a deputy. The sheriff, who had been slightly wounded, had killed one of the drifters; but the other two escaped, leaving the money behind in their panic.

Juan Tolosa had brought the news to Bailey with tears in his eyes. Juan's brother Miguel had been the third dead customer.

Bailey opened one eye far enough to see that his horse had carried him onto a plain that stretched several miles before it was broken by some large, low mesas. Although the land between Bailey and the mesas looked unbroken, he knew it was crisscrossed by arroyos, some of which were deep enough to hide a man and his horse. Bailey also knew that foolish men who had camped in arroyos had been drowned and washed away by flash floods. What he could see of the sky through his one partially opened eye showed no sign of rain though; and after passing through several arroyos, Bailey found one that would serve his purpose.

Before guiding his horse into it, Bailey looked back toward the butte. There was no sign of pursuit. Once in the arroyo, Bailey slid from his saddle. After pouring water from his canteen into his hat, he allowed his horse to drink. Then he took another sip himself before sinking into a sitting position with his back against the side of the arroyo.

"Congratulations, Bailey," Anne had said with her large, green eyes sparkling and a smile on her lips. Later that night after he had finished stammering as they had stood before the door to her parents' house, she had worn that same expression. "Yes, I'd be honored to be your wife," she had said. And then Anne had kissed him. Bailey couldn't remember walking back to the mercantile or climbing the stairs to the rooms where he and his father had lived. Bailey was sure he must have grinned all night in his sleep. In fact, he had grinned for the next four months—after he had adjusted to the deaths of his pa and Doc Atwood.

Bailey shook himself, struggled to his feet, and crawled up the side of the arroyo. As he looked toward the butte, his eyes refused to focus during the short periods of time that he could keep them open. He thought he could make out some kind of movement on the lower part of the butte, but he couldn't be sure. Then he began to have dry heaves. He slid back down the steep side of the arroyo and lay curled in a ball, massaging his temples with his fingertips.

When Bailey had run out of his medicine, which really did help his headaches most of the time, he had paid a visit to the town's new doctor, a young, pale, neatly dressed man from Illinois, who appeared to be not much older than Bailey. As they had shaken hands that day, the doctor had spoken first. "Isn't your name Bailey?" he had asked. After Bailey had answered him, the man had grown even paler and had asked him to sit down. The doctor had sat behind the small desk with his hands folded and resting on it. Staring at his hands instead of looking at Bailey's face, the pale doctor had spoken quietly. "I'm afraid I have some bad news, Mr. Bailey. I was going through some of Dr. Atwood's belongings yesterday when I discovered this letter. It is apparently a reply to an inquiry that he had made about several of his patients. It must have arrived only a day or two after Dr. Atwood's death and been laid aside without being opened."

The doctor had swallowed hard, glanced at Bailey's face, and then continued. "There's no easy way to say this. The doctor who wrote this letter believes that you probably have less than a month to live. There appears to be a problem with your—"

"Thanks, Doc," Bailey had said, holding up a hand as if to ward off a blow. "I don't savvy doctor talk enough to make it worth your while to explain. Do I owe you anything?"

After the young doctor had refused any kind of payment, Bailey had gone straight to his rooms over the mercantile. He had written a brief letter to Anne, telling her that he had been called away on business and reminding her that he loved her. Then he had written a second letter to Ed Lawson, a lawyer and good friend. He had revealed the young doctor's diagnosis and had asked him to make sure that the mercantile went to Anne after he was dead. He had given both of the letters to Billy Ramsbottom along with a silver dollar and instructions to wait an hour before he delivered them. Then after telling Abigail Cox, the widow he had hired to help tend the mercantile, that he didn't know when he'd be back, Bailey had saddled his horse and ridden off to die.

Bailey opened one eye when he heard a noise close to him. He couldn't focus, but he recognized the dark shape a few yards away. "Not yet, you dirty buzzard," he mumbled, pulling his six-shooter from its holster. "Not while I'm still alive." Bailey pulled the hammer back and took a deep breath to steady his shaking hand, raised the gun, and pulled the trigger.

Bailey had several vague, shadowy thoughts, but the next thing that came to him clearly was that he was lying on a bed and that people were whispering. As he lay there, his eyes still closed, he recognized Anne's voice.

"Dr. Loney, is he going to be all right?"

"Yes, Miss Anne. I'm so sorry about the confusion in names. I—"

"You're not to blame, Doctor. You've only been here for three weeks; that's hardly enough time to become acquainted with all of your patients and their ailments.

"Maybe, Ma'am, but I should have made sure I was talking to the right—"

"Didn't you ask him if his name was Bailey?"

"Yes, Ma'am, but—"

"And didn't he tell you it was?"

"Yes, Ma'am, but—"

"Shhh! I'm not going to let you blame yourself for something, you couldn't help. How could you have remembered if you had even discovered yet—that Doc Atwood had sent for a second opinion on several patients, including both Bailey O'Toole and Joe Bailey? Besides, you couldn't have prevented Joe's heart from stopping, could you?"

"No, Ma'am."

"And Bailey's going to be fine, isn't he?"

"Yes, Ma'am, he is—but no thanks to me. We'd never have spotted him in that arroyo if he hadn't taken a shot at those buzzards."

"True, but didn't you say that this other medicine that you gave him would do more for his headaches than what he had been taking?"

"It should," the doctor whispered, "but I can't be sure—"

"Yes, you can," Bailey said. He opened his eyes and propped himself on one elbow. "I still have a headache, but it's nothing like it was. Doc, don't be too hard on yourself. When you called me Mr. Bailey, if I had listened for a couple of minutes, I'd have known you were talking about someone else. Besides, you weren't completely wrong. I *am* going to die."

Bailey watched as the startled doctor grew pale and Anne gasped. He smiled and sat up. "I'm going to die of starvation. What does a man have to do to get something to eat around here?"

THE REWARD

Doctor Joseph Thomas Greenwood pulled a blood-speckled sheet over the face of Dave Yochim and looked into the tearful eyes of Dave's young widow.

"I'm sorry," he said.

"Don't be," she said. "You've nothing to be sorry for. Only God could have saved Dave." She took a deep breath and straightened her backbone. "Thank you for your help. I need to go to my children." She stood silent for a moment, looking at the floor. Then she raised her eyes to the doctor's face. "Joe, I've never made funeral arrangements before—" she buried her face in her hands and began to sob.

Circling the body, the doctor stood beside the grieving woman and put a comforting arm around her shoulder. "I'll take care of the arrangements, Laura; don't you fret."

He stood in the doorway and watched her take another deep breath before she stepped off the wooden sidewalk and crossed the dusty street toward Mrs. London's boarding house. Her two children—four-year-old Linda and six-year-old Billy—had been taken there after the shooting.

"Yes, Ma'am," he said softly. "I'll take care of the arrangements."

Later that night Doc Greenwood sat at a small table in the room above his office. He propped an elbow on the table; and with his chin resting on one hand, he looked at the quiet, empty street below. "It makes no sense," he said. "They had no reason to kill him."

Dave Yochim had been liked by everyone who had known him. He had loaded his family in the buckboard that morning and driven the six miles from his small ranch to celebrate a successful cattle drive and to pay off a loan at the bank across the street. He had planned to pick up some supplies at Johnson's Dry Goods Store and then treat his family to one of Mrs. London's delicious meals. He hadn't planned on walking into the bank while Joshua and Jonathan Riddle were robbing it.

According to the bank's president, Dave hadn't even reached for his gun. Joshua Riddle had just shot him out of meanness. Then as he had taken the money from Dave's body, Joshua had smiled. Jonathan, the younger of the two, had cursed his brother, but the damage had been done. They had stuffed the money into their saddlebags and had galloped away before anyone had had a chance to react. Dave had been dead before he'd hit the floor.

Doc blew out his lamp and stretched out on his bed, but sleep wouldn't come. Somewhere past three o'clock, he sprang out of bed and lit the lamp. He sat once again at the table, and with a stubby pencil he wrote four names on a scrap of paper. Ten minutes later he was sleeping soundly with a slight smile on his lips. In spite of a rough night, Doc got up the next morning at 5:30. After eating his breakfast at Mrs.London's as usual, he went to the sheriff's office.

"Is there a reward for Josh Riddle?" he asked, after greeting the sheriff cordially.

"There's three thousand on him and two thousand on his brother since the last robbery. Counting Dave, the Riddles have killed at least six men and one woman. Why, Doc, you're not thinking of going after them two, are you?"

"No," Doc said, "I'm just taking care of some arrangements." He pulled the scrap of paper from a vest pocket, handed it to the sheriff, and asked, "Can you think of anyone around here who's better at his work than the first man on this list?"

The sheriff looked from the paper to the doctor in surprise. "No," he said, "but what do you want with a man like him? He's a half-breed and—"

"I'm obliged, Sheriff. Do you know if he's in town?"

"He is unless he broke out of jail," the sheriff said. "I locked him up late last night for disturbing the peace. He's sleeping off the whiskey in a cell right now."

"Could I talk to him?" Doc asked.

Fifteen minutes later, when Doc stepped out of the sheriff 's office, he was rubbing his palms together and grinning. He pulled the scrap of paper from his vest pocket and crossed off the first name.

"One," he muttered.

Nearly a month had passed before a tinker Doc had been watching for finally came through town again. They talked for an hour before reaching an agreement. Money changed hands, and the tinker drove his cart to the doctor's back door. As the tinker drove away, Doc pulled his scrap of paper from a pocket and crossed another name off his list.

"Two," he said.

After that night Doc began leaving the door to his room unlocked when he went to bed.

Two nights later, he crossed the third name off his list as he watched a rider disappear into the darkness of the alley that passed his back door.

"Three," he mumbled as he climbed the stairs to his room.

When Doc awoke in the middle of the night eight nights later, he knew that he wasn't alone.

"You the doc?" someone asked in a raspy whisper. When Doc sat up, he felt a gun barrel poke his ribs.

"Yes. What's wrong?"

"Get dressed and come with me," replied the visitor.

In the darkness Doc smiled.

The sheriff looked up from a newspaper in surprise when Doc walked in. He struggled to his feet and came around his cluttered desk, his large belly jiggling with each step.

"Where have you been for the past four days, Doc? The whole town has been worried since you disappeared."

Doc tilted his hat back and smiled. "I'm sorry Bob; I was called away in the middle of the night to a camp about twenty miles north of here. It was a strange case—two men had been poisoned and were in pretty bad shape. I did what I could, but in the end they both killed themselves. There I was, stuck with two corpses. I did what I had to do."

"You buried 'em proper?" the sheriff asked. Without thinking about his action, he removed his hat.

"No, I brought their bodies to town so that I could claim the reward," Doc replied. "The two men were Joshua and Jonathan Riddle."

The sheriff stared at the doctor in disbelief. Then he shuffled out the door. Holding his bandana over his mouth and nose, he examined the two blanket- wrapped corpses that were draped over the horses at the hitching post. Not until he had stumbled back into his office, slumped into his chair, and taken a long drink from a whiskey bottle he kept in his desk, did the sheriff speak again.

"How did you happen to be the one they came after?" asked the sheriff. He shook his head and whistled softly. "What incredible luck! You've got five thousand dollars coming, Doc!"

"There wasn't much luck involved, Bob," said Doc. He took a seat on the opposite side of the desk. "I earned that money. Do you remember a couple of months ago when I talked to Breed McKinlay in one of your cells?"

"Sure, but what does that have to do with this?"

Doc smiled. "Everything—I hired him to track the Riddles and find out where their hideout was. He found it, and I sent Peter Wedell out there—"

"The tinker?" the sheriff asked.

"Yep," Doc replied. "I loaded a keg of special whiskey on his cart and told him to get close enough to the Riddles' camp to attract their attention so that they'd either buy or steal that whiskey. I don't know which they did because Pete kept going on his circuit, but they got it, and they drank it, and they got real sick."

Leaning forward in his chair, the sheriff asked, "Now wait a minute, Doc. How could you be sure they'd come and get you to help? They did, didn't they? That was luck!"

"Yes, they came and got me; but no, it wasn't luck," replied Doc. He was still smiling. "I paid Dick Austin, the most harmless-looking old timer and the best liar I could find, to set up camp near enough to the Riddle boys that they could see his fire at night. When they came to him for help, he sent Jonathan to me and offered to stay with Josh, who was already pretty sick."

The sheriff leaned back in his chair, his mouth open and his eyes wide. "Doc, you mean to say you as good as murdered them two hombres? Ain't that against some oath you doctors take?"

As Doc leaned across the sheriff 's desk, he looked more like a lawyer than a doctor. "I didn't kill them," he said. "What I gave them in their whiskey was large doses of emetics and laxatives that doctors have used for years to expel poisons. The medical terms for what I did to them are 'puking' and 'purging.'"

"Then why'd they kill theirselves?" asked the sheriff.

"Well, Bob," Doc replied, "after Jonathan had taken me to their hideout and I had examined them—Jonathan was mighty sick by then too, and I encouraged them both to have some more whiskey for medicinal purposes—I told them that I was pretty sure they had cholera. I also told them that I was pretty sure that there was nothing I could do for them. Then I described what an awful death awaited them. I left them and went with Dick to get more wood for the fire. We heard two shots and found them dead. Dick helped me tie their bodies to their horses and rode back to town with me. He's probably in the saloon, spending his pay."

The sheriff shook his head in disbelief. "Well, if that don't beat all!"

"Oh, by the way," Doc continued, "most of the bank's money is in my saddlebags. When the reward money comes, I'll take a hundred dollars to cover my expenses. Give the rest to Laura Yochim."

"That's mighty generous of you, Doc." The sheriff grunted as he struggled to his feet. "What should I tell her about the money?" he asked.

Doc, on his way out the door, said over his shoulder, "Tell her I made the necessary arrangements." Closing the door behind him, Doc looked at Josh Riddle's body, still draped over the saddle. Taking a scrap of paper and a stubby pencil from his vest pocket, he drew a neat line through a name. He muttered as he started across the street toward Mrs. London's place, "Four."

THE SPITOON

I'm a private kind of man. I don't make a habit of poking my nose into other folks' business, and I'm obliged when they stay out of mine. I'm not unfriendly, and I try not to be unpleasant, but some people just don't know when to quit. When the loud man flung the bat-wing doors open and stomped into the saloon, I reckoned he was one of those people.

I was sitting at a table in the back corner with my back to the wall. Less than half an hour earlier I had ridden into Bisbee, Arizona. After two weeks of riding from sunup to sundown to get there, I was tired of beans and jerky. I was tired of washing particles of sand from my mouth with the brackish water from my canteen. I was tired of sweating all day and sleeping on rocky ground. Almost thirty years as a cowboy, Pony Express rider, and Texas Ranger had accustomed me to discomfort; they had not made me fond of it.

On the table in front of me sat my supper: a large, juicy steak; four big, fluffy sourdough biscuits; a bowl of peaches; and a cup of the best coffee I had tasted in months. All I wanted was to be left alone to enjoy my meal. Now I was pretty sure that I was about to be interrupted. Keeping my attention on my plate, I decided to put away as much of my meal as I could. Besides, maybe the loud man wouldn't pay any mind to me.

"Hey, Grandpa!" he said. Ignoring him, I continued to eat.

"I guess the old man must be deaf!" he said. The two cowboys who had come in with him, smaller rags torn from the same bolt of cloth, laughed.

"Maybe you should speak up, big brother," one of them said.

"Or move a little closer, Del," the other added.

I poured a second cup of steaming coffee from the pot that the bartender had left for me. Still looking at my plate, I bit into a biscuit.

"I ain't getting any closer," said Del. "That old man stinks bad enough from here."

Again, there was laughter. He was right about one thing; I didn't smell very good. Riding straight through town to the livery stable, I had unsaddled Midnight and paid the stable boy to rub him down and give him a double helping of oats. I had stopped at the hotel, paid for a room, and left my gear there. On my way out, I had asked the clerk to recommend an eating place. Before leaving, I had ordered a bath to be ready in an hour. Then I had come here to enjoy my supper.

I ate another piece of steak so tender I could almost cut it with my fork. As I chewed, I closed my eyes and anticipated soaking my tired, aching body in a tub of hot water while smoking one of the stogies I had tucked away in my saddlebags.

"Shhhh—I think Grandpa has dozed off," said Del. "Matt, he just might fall into his plate and smother hisself. Maybe you better wake him up."

I heard the distinct sound of someone cocking a Colt. A nearly deafening explosion followed; and I could feel the bullet smash into the floor a few inches from my boot, showering my pant leg with splinters. As I glanced in their direction, Matt, who appeared to be the youngest of the three, spun his six-shooter on his finger and slipped it smoothly into his holster.

"Grandpa," said Del, "I reckon you ought to thank Matt here for saving your life. I would have asked Tony to wake you up; but he's such a bad shot, he might have hit you."

I knew they weren't going to go away, but I wasn't about to give up my supper because these rowdy boys wanted some entertainment. They appeared to be more bored than bad. I took another bite of biscuit and washed it down with a swig of coffee. Saluting them with my cup, I smiled.

"I'm obliged, Matt, for keeping me awake," I said. "I'm mighty tired right now. I'm obliged to you, too, Del, for picking the best shot to do the honors. Why, who could tell by looking that he's the one that can shoot straight enough to hit the floor?"

I had another bite of steak while the brothers digested what I had said.

"I think that old man is making fun of us," said Tony, taking a step forward.

"Hold on," said Del, placing a hand on his brother's shoulder. "Old man, are you trying to make fools of us?"

"Now, that would be closing the corral gate after the horses were gone, wouldn't it?" I asked.

"What horses?" Matt whispered.

I buttered another biscuit, took a bite, and then cut off another piece of steak. Del was about to speak, but I cut him off. "I'm saying my dear, departed grandmother could have made that shot from twice as far away and without her spectacles. But then you weren't wearing yours either."

"Matt don't wear spectacles," Del said.

"Maybe he needs to," I said, sipping more coffee.

"Del, he is making fun of us," said Tony. "Can I—"

"I'll take care of this," said Del, his hand resting on the butt of his Colt. "You got some mouth on you, Grandpa," he said.

"Thank you," I said. I finished my biscuit and began to butter another one.

"Stand up!" Del said.

"Can't," I said.

"What did you say?" he asked.

"Can't!" I said, nearly shouting. Taking a bite of steak, I shook my head. "Matt's eyes are bad, and Del's hard of hearing. Is anything wrong with you, Tony?"

Leaning with his back against the bar and his thumbs hooked in his gun belt, Tony focused his attention on raking the floor with his spur. "Well, sometimes when the thunder and lightning gets real bad, I—"

"Shut up, Tony!" said Del. "Grandpa, I told you to stand up."

"Can't," I said.

"Why not—are your knees knocking too bad?" Del asked.

"Nope," I said, chewing a large piece of steak and gesturing at the table with my fork. "I'm eating my supper, and I like to eat sitting down when I can."

Three explosions followed so quickly that they sounded more like one long roar in the room. A small cloud of smoke drifted toward the ceiling. Brushing splinters from my pants, I glanced at the bullet holes in the floor. I shook my head slowly and looked at Del, who was still holding his Colt.

"Granny shot like that one time," I said. "Shut herself in her cabin for a week—wouldn't talk to anybody for the pure shame of it. Bar keep says he's got some dried apple pie in the kitchen. You wouldn't happen to know if it's any good, would you?"

"Yes, Sir," said Matt. "I have a piece pretty near every time I'm in town—"

"Shut up!" Del said. "I hit what I'm aiming at, old man."

I buttered my last biscuit, laid my knife across the edge of my plate, and then took a silver dollar from my vest pocket. Holding it up, I asked, "Del, are you a gambler?"

Del looked confused. "What are you getting at?"

I smiled and laid the dollar on the edge of the table. "That dollar says you're not a good enough shot to move the spittoon at the end of the bar twice without putting a hole in it."

"I only get two shots?" he asked, squinting at the spittoon.

"Yep," I said. I drank what was left of my coffee and then refilled my cup. I put another piece of steak in my mouth and chewed slowly.

When Del's first slug hit the floor close enough to rock the spittoon slightly, I gave him a nod. His second shot was too far to the left. He holstered his Colt and flipped me a dollar, which I caught and laid on top of the first one.

"Want to try for double or nothing, Matt?" I asked. "You get four shots to move it three times."

"I don't mind taking an old man's money," Matt said, smiling. "Let me get your dollar back for you, big Brother." He drew smoothly and fired.

"Looks like one of us is going to be buying a new spittoon," I said.

"You talk too much, Grandpa," said Matt, taking deliberate aim and squeezing the trigger. The spittoon scooted two inches, nearly turning over. His third shot moved it again.

The barkeep, standing behind the bar at the same end as the brothers, had been silently polishing glasses and stacking them within easy reach, stopping occasionally to pour more whiskey for them. "Someone will have to pay for it," he mumbled.

"Loser pays for the spittoon," said Del, smiling, I reckon, at the idea of getting his money back.

"Fair enough," I replied. I brushed the two silver dollars off the table just before Matt fired. It wasn't much of a distraction, but it was enough. Matt's face reddened as he holstered his gun. "You did that on purpose, Old Man!"

"Sorry to be so clumsy," I said, stooping to retrieve the coins. "Tell you what I'll do though, boys; I'll call off that bet and make the same bet with Tony. All he has to do is hit the spittoon three of five times. It's ruined anyway. What do you say?"

Del and Matt looked at each other and then at Tony. "You got the two dollars, Tony?" Del asked.

"Come on, Del," said Tony, a trace of a whine in his voice. "I can do it—I know I can! Just give me a chance!"

I used that last biscuit to soak up some of the juice from the steak. Wiping my mouth with a cloth napkin, I leaned back in my chair and smiled.

"You'd better hit the danged thing!" said Del, giving Tony a shove that put him two feet closer to the spittoon. I noticed that Tony's brothers stepped behind him as he drew his gun, and I wondered if I should move. I was, after all, only a dozen feet to the left of the spittoon. I had reckoned that Del had exaggerated about how bad Tony's shooting was, but he hadn't. The one time he did hit the spittoon, his thumb slipped on the hammer, causing him to fire before he had taken time to aim. Head hanging, Tony turned to the bar and finished his drink.

"Here, Mister," he said. He turned from the bar and shuffled toward me, holding out a handful of coins. "You win."

"Wait a minute!" said Del, grabbing Tony's shoulder. "This old man has stole all the money from us he's going to—in fact, I'm going to take back my dollar and his too." As he started toward me, each brother grabbed one of Del's arms.

"We agreed to the bet, Del," said Matt, "and we lost. Pay the man, Tony."

As Tony let go of his brother's arm and started toward me, Del's head drooped; and his shoulders sagged. He must have felt Matt's grip relax because suddenly Del tore free. Jumping to his left, the big man leveled his Colt at my chest.

Sipping coffee, I studied him over the rim of my cup. "Barkeep," I said, smiling, "I'm ready for pie."

"Don't get between us, Tony," said Del. "Just keep walking to the side and get them two dollars. Bring them back here and give them to me."

"Del," said Tony, "I don't want no trouble. Why don't we—"

"Move!" Del said.

"Del," I said, "listen to Tony. You don't want trouble. I want to show you something very special, and then we'll see if you still want the money. May I? I'm going to move very slowly so you can see what I'm doing." With my thumb and forefinger, I pulled my own Colt from its holster and laid it on the table.

Matt's spurs jingled as he stepped to Del's side. The three stood in a rough semicircle in front of my table with Tony standing a step or two closer to me.

"It looks like a plain old Colt to me," said Del. "What's so special about it?"

"It has something your guns don't have," I said. I picked it up with my right hand and cocked it, keeping the barrel pointed at the ceiling.

Instantly Matt and Tony drew their guns and pointed them at me. Del chuckled. "I don't care what it has," he said. "That Colt of yours is outnumbered three to one, Grandpa. Now, just for fun, tell us—what does it have that ours don't?"

I motioned to the barkeep, who started toward the kitchen. "Bullets, Del," I said. I smiled at them. "You boys light a shuck. I have some pie to eat, a bath to take, and a cigar to smoke." I extended my left hand toward Tony for the coins. "I'm much obliged to you for the entertainment and for the supper which you have so generously provided. I'll be happy to recommend your hospitality to others if you wish; but if not, I'll never breathe a word of what happened here today."

They shuffled from the room without looking back. The barkeep set a huge piece of dried apple pie on the table in front of me. Holstering my Colt, I ate my pie in peace. Matt had been right; the pie was good. I reckoned the bath and the stogie would be good too.

THE SWITCH

Scott Martin leaned back in the train-compartment seat, hat pulled over his eyes, one arm draped over his carpetbag, apparently asleep. He was actually wide awake, and at the moment he was scrutinizing the two other passengers who sat facing him.

The man, wearing a neat black suit with a red brocade vest, looked to be fifty. He had steel gray eyes; a hawk nose; a thin, neatly trimmed white moustache; and a crop of thick, white hair. Long, sinewy hands held the flat-brimmed Stetson in his lap.

Seated on his left was a beautiful young lady that Scott guessed must have been seventeen or eighteen. Her thick, black hair, piled high on her head, set off her pale skin, rosy cheeks, and large, blue eyes. She reminded Scott of a doll he had seen in a store window in Abilene several months ago.

The old man was dozing at that moment, his sagging head moving with the swaying of the train. The young lady was looking at Scott with a mixture of curiosity and apprehension. She wore an attractive dress that pretty much matched the color of her eyes.

No threat to me, Scott thought to himself. Closing his eyes, he decided to try to sleep while he could. Things couldn't have gone better for him. For three weeks he had studied the routine at the Cattleman's Bank in Casa Grande. He had watched the procedure when large amounts of money were deposited or withdrawn, and he had carefully planned each step he would take.

When the time had come, he had been ready. The three or four people who had watched the whole thing hadn't raised an alarm because they hadn't been aware of what had happened. Even the bank employee who'd been carrying the money hadn't guessed that he'd been robbed. Scott smiled slightly as he visualized the bank clerk giving his version of what had happened.

"Well, I was taking the money out to put it in the strong box on the company stage," he would begin. "Just as I came through the door, an eastern dude came running down the sidewalk, knocking me flatter than a flapjack. He apologized, helped me up, brushed me off, and handed me my bag. Poor fellow was hunting the doctor— said his wife was having a baby in their hotel room. I tried to calm him down, and I showed him the way to Doc Windham's office. He picked up his bag and went tearing off down the sidewalk again— probably his first baby."

Half an hour later, Scott awoke to the impact of another human body slamming into his. Startled, he grabbed for his gun but then realized that the train had braked hard and catapulted his fellow passengers from their seats.

They must have been asleep too, thought Scott, judging from the bewildered look on the old man's face.

The man, seated directly across from Scott, had landed squarely in Scott's lap. The girl had been thrown to the floor and had struck her head. A knot was swelling on her forehead, and blood trickled from the center of the knot.

After helping the old man, who apologized repeatedly, Scott turned to the girl. "Are you all right, Ma'am?" he asked.

Placing her small, white hand to her forehead and feeling the knot, she replied in a rather shaky voice. "W—What happened?"

"Probably cattle on the tracks," Scott replied. He took her hand in his and pulled her to her feet. She pulled a handkerchief from her bag and wiped the blood from her forehead as the train began to pick up speed again.

"Thank you, Mr.—"

"Smith," he said.

She smiled. "Thank you, Mr. Smith. Papa, are you hurt?"

"No," the old man replied, "Mr. Smith is the one who should be hurt. I landed on him."

Scott smiled at them. "I don't reckon you broke anything," he said.

"I'm afraid we've been a bit rude, Mr. Smith," the man said. "We should have introduced ourselves, but we don't travel much, and you being a stranger and all, we thought—well, never mind all that. I'm Jake Saunders, and this is my daughter Linda. Please forgive our bad manners. A person just has to be careful these days."

"I understand," said Scott.

"We're headed for Tucson; I've come out here for my health. Linda came along to keep an eye on me. What about you, Mr. Smith?"

After a brief conversation, the old man and the girl both began to doze again. Pulling his hat back down to shade his eyes, Scott thought about how clever he had been when he had "borrowed" that drummer's clothes so that people would remember a "dude" who had run past the bank. Now he wore a faded blue shirt and black jeans, his own brown Stetson, and a pair of worn but clean boots. No one could identify him as the man at the bank. He was in the clear.

When the train stopped for an hour at Tucson, Scott got off with his traveling companions to stretch his legs and say goodbye. Jake disappeared for a few minutes, but Scott sat and visited with Linda until Jake returned. When the conductor called, Scott shook hands with the old man, tipped his hat to Linda, and stepped onto the platform at the rear of his car.

"It's been my pleasure, Folks."

Jake lifted his hat, and Linda waved as the train began to move.

"This will help you pass the time while you travel," Jake said, holding out a folded piece of paper, which Scott put in his shirt pocket.

Probably one of those Bible thumper's tracts, he thought. He made his way to his empty compartment and tossed his carpet bag on the seat. He sprawled out, trying to get comfortable. The train wouldn't reach Wilcox until morning; and he wasn't hungry, so he might as well get some sleep.

The carpet bag beneath his head was terribly uncomfortable. He thought of the stacks of bills inside it. He had only risked looking at them once, in his hotel room when he had transferred them from the bank bag to his plain, common carpet bag. He was surprised at how hard those bundles felt when he rested his head on them.

"Must be where the term *hard cash* came from," he said. He chuckled as he sat up and looked around. No one was watching. He could take another look at his loot without being seen. He unbuckled the leather straps that kept the bag closed, reached in, and pulled out a book. Scott stared at it stupidly for a moment. He thrust his hand into the bag again and extracted another book. Then he inverted the bag, spilling its contents on the seat beside him. There was no money; there were only books.

Scott was stunned. The bag he had carried from his hotel room had never left his sight. He had kept it with him everywhere he had gone. He had slept with his arms around it. With his own hands, he had put the money into the bag; but now the money was gone.

Suddenly, Scott thought of the paper Jake Saunders had handed him. Absently he pulled it from his pocket and found that it bore his assumed name. Quickly he unfolded the paper and read the neatly written words.

Dear Mr. Smith,

By one of those strange coincidences of life, my daughter and I were crossing the street this morning when you robbed the bank. We witnessed your exchange of bags with the bank clerk. Since I have been the president and owner of that bank for the past ten years, I felt that I had an obligation to protect the investments of my customers.

Knowing the approximate weight of the money you stole, I prepared a similar bag by putting into it about the same weight in books. You see, I didn't want you to be left with nothing of value.

After talking to you on the train, I reckoned you are too intelligent and good-hearted to rot away in prison. I observed your intelligence in the way you planned and executed your robbery, and your kindness when you helped us on the train. I'm sure you realize by now that we arranged that sudden stop. Your concern for us was genuine—genuine to the degree that it distracted you while Linda repeated your exchange of bags. For these reasons I have decided to satisfy myself with the return of my bank's money and to let you go. If you can come to me one year from today with proof that you have given up all thoughts of a life of crime, I will be happy to give you a job. Until then I remain your servant,

Jake Saunders

Scott Martin smiled, folded the letter, and put it back in his shirt pocket. When the train stopped in the next town, he got off long enough to send a telegram.

Mr. Jake Saunders, president of the Cattleman's Bank in Casa Grande,

Hold a position, will be there one year from today. I am much obliged.

Scott Martin

He returned to the train and made himself comfortable. Smiling, he selected a book from the carpetbag, settled back, and began to read.

THE EDGE

Thomas Jefferson Wilcox removed his Stetson and wiped the sweat from its inside leather band with his bandanna. Then he wiped his forehead and replaced the Stetson, pulling its brim down so that it shaded his eyes. After tying his bandana loosely around his neck, he sipped tepid water from his nearly empty canteen, swirled it briefly in his mouth, and spat it to his left. Leaning forward in the saddle, he rested his hands on the horn and watched the quiet little town that lay half a mile ahead and slightly below him. He brushed away a fly and then pulled the makings from a vest pocket, rolled a cigarette, scratched a match on his leg, and held the flame to the tobacco.

As he smoked, he continued to watch the town. Holding his cigarette between his lips, he pulled a folded paper from another vest pocket. He unfolded the wrinkled paper and read the familiar words aloud, his cigarette waving with each syllable. "Wanted: Thomas 'Kid' Wilcox, $50 Reward."

Shaking his head slowly, he folded the paper without reading the rest of it and tucked it back into his pocket. "Fifty dollars," he said. "I can do better than that." After taking a final drag on his cigarette, he flicked it to the ground. "I reckon somebody in this little hole-in-the-wall town can oblige me by letting me take his money at gunpoint."

Kid Wilcox dismounted. Still holding the reins in his left hand, he took two deliberate steps in front of his horse. With his right hand, in one swift, smooth move, he drew his six-shooter from its holster.

He replaced the gun, flexed his fingers, and drew it again. This time, before he holstered the gun, he checked the cartridges. He turned the cylinder slowly until he came to the empty chamber that he kept under the hammer when he was on the trail. Removing a cartridge from one of the loops on his gun belt, he inspected it briefly, blew on it to remove any dust, and slid it into the chamber. He dropped the gun into its holster, swung into the saddle, and started his mustang down the gentle slope toward the town.

Kid Wilcox had not decided to rob the mercantile in this particular town on this particular day on a whim. He was not one of those ignorant outlaws who rode into a random town, tried to rob a bank or a stage office, and got himself arrested or shot. He had been watching this town for almost a month. Twice he had ridden into town for a closer look. The first time he had bought supplies at the mercantile and exchanged small talk with the skinny little bald man who owned it. On his second visit, the Kid had cleverly directed the conversation to get the owner to brag about what a good business the mercantile was doing.

"What this town needs is a bank," the man had said. "The closest bank is in Benson, so we do our own banking for the most part. We get over to Benson about once a month to deposit money if we need to."

Kid Wilcox smiled as he remembered how he had pretended to have no interest in what the owner had been telling him. Before he had left the mercantile, though, he had learned that the owner had not been to Benson for two weeks. Two more weeks had passed since that day. The mercantile's till should be full.

The Kid had discovered that the town lacked not only a bank but also a sheriff 's office. An old timer, who seemed to do nothing but doze in a rocking chair on the veranda that spanned the width of the mercantile, had revealed that there was no law in the town. On his second visit, the Kid had been leaning against the veranda rail, enjoying the shade and a cigarette.

"We're peaceful folks," the old timer had muttered through his bushy white mustache. "We don't have much trouble in our town."

"What happens if you do have trouble?" the Kid had asked.

"We deal with it," the old timer had replied.

Now as the Kid walked his horse past the livery stable, he could see the old timer sitting in his usual place. "Let's see you deal with this, Old Timer," he muttered.

He dismounted and tied the reins loosely to the hitching rail in front of the mercantile. A woman with two young children was coming through the doorway as he started up the steps. When the Kid smiled and touched the brim of his Stetson, the woman smiled back at him. She was carrying several packages, and he wondered if he should thank her for the money she had added to the till.

The Kid paused in the doorway for several seconds to let his eyes adjust to the darker interior of the mercantile. The skinny bald man was wiping sweat from his head and neck with a faded red bandanna. He smiled when he saw the Kid. After tucking the bandana into a back pocket, he leaned forward with both hands on the counter and smiled.

"Howdy, Pardner, what can I do for you today?" he asked.

The Kid smiled back at him. "Got an empty flour sack?" he asked.

"I got a dozen of 'em," replied the bald man. He reached under the counter, pulled out a neatly folded flour sack, and laid it on the counter. "You just need one?"

"I reckon one will be enough," the Kid said. "Now, I need a couple of tins of peaches, two pounds of coffee, and two pounds of beans."

The skinny little bald man filled the Kid's order, placing the items on the counter beside the sack. "Need more tobacco and papers yet?" he asked.

The kid slipped a hand into his vest pocket and grinned. "I reckon I do," he said. "I'm obliged."

The skinny bald man smiled as he placed the papers on the counter. "You're welcome," he said. "Need anything else?"

The Kid smiled. "I'd like all the money in your till," he said.

The skinny bald man laughed. "You have a great sense of humor, Pardner," he said.

"I'm not joking," the Kid said. "Put the money and the supplies in the sack, and hand it over."

The skinny bald man's smile disappeared. "You don't want to do this," he said. "There's a lot of money in the till, I—"

"Enough to die trying to keep it?" the Kid asked. Almost as if by magic, his six-shooter appeared in his hand. "Put the money in the sack and be quick about it."

"I was starting to like you," the skinny bald man said. He sounded more sad than angry.

The Kid grinned as he grabbed the sack and backed away from the counter. "I still like you, Mister," he said. "I don't want any harm to come to you, so I'm asking you to keep quiet until I'm out of town. I don't want to have to leave you hogtied and gagged. You savvy?"

The skinny bald man nodded.

The Kid holstered his six-shooter and continued backing toward the door. He had almost reached it when something occurred to him. He pulled the folded paper from his vest pocket and sauntered back to the counter. Still smiling, the Kid unfolded the "wanted" poster with his free hand and placed it on the counter. "When the law shows up asking questions, make sure you get the name right," the Kid said. Again, he backed toward the door. When he reached it, he turned and stepped onto the veranda.

The Kid had taken one step toward his horse when a sound from his left stopped him. In the quiet of the afternoon, the sound had been easy to identify. Someone had pulled the hammer back on a gun. As the Kid turned his head in the direction of the sound, he instinctively reached for his six-shooter. He froze when he saw the business end of a double-barreled shotgun pointed at him.

"Your choice, Boy," the old timer said. "Make the right choice, and you'll live to make others. Make the wrong choice, and, well, a shotgun like this can make a real mess of a man. Just set your sack down, and then unbuckle your gun belt, and toss it into the street."

The old timer was still seated in his rocking chair. He was leaning forward, aiming the short-barreled coach gun at the Kid. "I know what you're thinking," he said. "You're younger and faster than I am. But I pulled back both hammers, and these triggers have a mighty light touch to them. Face it, Boy; I have the edge on you."

Slowly the Kid set the sack on the boardwalk and untied the leather thong that circled his thigh. Muttering a curse, he unbuckled his gun belt and tossed it onto the edge of the dusty street.

"Now, here's my plan," said the old timer. As he stood stiffly and stretched his back, he kept the coach gun pointed at the Kid. "Pay close attention because if you deviate from my plan—well, I reckon one of us will be real sorry. Step over by your horse so Sam can fetch his money without being in the line of fire."

Still muttering curses, the Kid obeyed. He watched the skinny bald man shuffle out to pick up the sack.

"You should be ashamed of yourself," he said. "I really was starting to like you, you young whelp." Shaking his bald head, the skinny man handed the wanted poster to the old timer and then retreated into his mercantile.

The old timer continued talking as if there had been no interruption. "You and I are riding over to Benson, where I'll turn you over to the town marshal so he can lock you in his jail until the circuit judge comes to town."

A blond-haired boy led a large roan mare down the street. The old timer walked around the Kid, still keeping the coach gun aimed at him. He took the reins from the boy and then swung into the saddle with a groan.

"Thanks, Billy," he said.

He glanced at the poster, folded it with one hand, and then slipped it into his vest pocket. "So, you're Kid Wilcox," he said. "Mount up, Kid Wilcox; and let's ride. I reckon we can make Benson in three hours. Walk your horse ahead of me; and please, don't try anything stupid. You already made one mistake today; another one like the first might cut the reward in half."

"What do you mean?" the Kid asked.

"I mean," the old timer said, "whoever put up this reward might have second thoughts as to whether or not you're worth fifty dollars." He chuckled. "Granted, I had an edge; but you were almighty easy to apprehend. I'm feeling a little guilty about accepting fifty dollars for so little effort."

Kid Wilcox twisted in his saddle to look at the old timer. "You don't have me in Benson yet," he said. "That scattergun may give you an edge for now, but it don't mean you'll keep that edge. A lot could happen between here and Benson, Old Man."

"I can't argue with you there," the old timer said. "I'm riding with my finger inside the trigger guard on this coach gun. My horse could step in a prairie dog hole, flinch from a rattler; or I could doze off in the saddle and then jerk when I woke up. I don't recollect whether that dodger said you could be brought in dead or alive—do you?"

Despite the heat from the mid-morning sun, the Kid felt a cold shiver run down his spine. The old timer rode two horse lengths behind him. He was gripping the coach gun in his right hand and resting the stock on his left forearm while holding the reins in his left hand. The Kid swallowed a lump in his throat.

"There's no need to keep your finger on the trigger, Old Man," he said. "You don't need to keep that thing pointed at my back either." He let out his breath slowly as the old timer swung the barrels upward and rested the butt of the coach gun on his right thigh. As he turned to face forward again, the Kid noticed that the old timer had kept his finger inside the trigger guard.

They rode without speaking for nearly half an hour. The Kid watched for an opportunity to escape the old timer, but the country was too open. His hands were free. He thought about whipping off his Stetson and waving it in the face of the old timer's horse. The horse would spook and throw its rider, allowing him to make a run for it. In a few seconds he could be out of range for the coach gun. The old timer wasn't wearing a six shooter, and he had left the Kid's with the skinny bald man. Maybe the fall would kill the old timer.

The Kid glanced over his shoulder and gritted his teeth. The old timer was too far behind to risk trying anything yet. He would have to be patient.

"Having an edge is a wonderful thing," the old timer said. "Have you ever had an edge, Kid Wilcox—I mean, have you ever had an edge because you planned to have it?"

The Kid ignored the question. He didn't want to have a conversation with this old coot.

"This dodger on you says you're wanted for armed robbery," the old timer said. "Did you plan that robbery better than you planned this one, or did you just get lucky?"

The Kid said nothing. He had planned his first robbery the same way he had planned this one, and he had gotten away with no problem. The only reason the owner of that mercantile had known his name was that the Kid had told him on the way out the door. The Kid smiled as he remembered how the pale little man had trembled and then wet himself. That robbery had gotten the Kid's life of crime started—even though it had only put sixty-eight dollars and two bits in his pocket. That amount of money wasn't a fortune, but it was almost the equivalent of three month's wages for long hours of back-breaking work on his father's ranch.

"Sure is hot," the old timer said. "Makes a man thankful for a full canteen, doesn't it? By the way, Kid Wilcox, help yourself to a drink from your canteen whenever you've a mind to. I wouldn't shoot a man for trying to quench his thirst. You did fill your canteen before attempting this robbery, didn't you?"

The Kid closed his eyes and muttered a curse. He hadn't thought about his canteen. He'd made a careless mistake. Then a thought occurred to him. This could be his chance to escape. He stopped his horse and looked over his shoulder at the old timer.

"I made a mistake, Old Man," he said. "I'd be obliged if you'd let me have a drink from your canteen."

The old timer chuckled, reined in his horse, and shook his head. "I'm sure you would," he said. "You'd be so obliged that when I got close enough, you'd try to knock me off my horse, take my canteen and light a shuck out of here."

"I need water!" the Kid said.

"I reckon you do," the old timer said, "but you're not getting a drop of mine."

"Are you going to let me die of thirst?"

"Nope." The old timer smiled. "You can drink from your own canteen."

"It's empty!"

"No," said the old timer, "it's full. While you were trying to rob the mercantile, I had Billy check your canteen. When he discovered that it was almost empty, I had him fill it. I reckon someone had to look out for you."

The Kid lifted his canteen and found it full. He took a long drink and muttered another curse as he hung his canteen on the saddle horn.

"You're welcome," the old timer said.

The two men had ridden without speaking for something like an hour when the Kid removed his Stetson and wiped the sweat from his face with his bandana. Glancing over his shoulder, he saw that his chance had come. The old timer was slumped in his saddle, his head bowed. He still held the shotgun in his right hand with the butt resting on his thigh and the barrels pointed upward.

The Kid tugged gently on the reins, and his horse stopped. All he had to do was to wait until the old timer pulled even with him. Then he could either knock the old man from his saddle or jerk the shotgun from his hands. When the Kid glanced over his shoulder again, he muttered another curse. The old timer's horse had stopped too, leaving a gap of four or five yards between the two animals. With another movement of the reins, the Kid began to back his horse toward the old timer. He stared in disbelief as the old timer's horse took a step backwards to match each step his own horse took.

"Kinda frustrating, ain't it?" the old man said. He straightened in his saddle and stretched his back muscles. Then he patted his horse's neck and chuckled. "In the days when I was a lawman, Buck and I brought in quite a few desperados. Sometimes we had to herd them for several days, and I got tired. I might have three or four men riding ahead of me, just watching for a chance to jump me."

The old timer uncorked his canteen and took a drink from it, replaced the cork, and then hung it by its strap over his saddle horn again.

"So, I trained Buck to keep his distance from any horse we were trailing. I reckon Buck adds to my edge, doesn't he?"

The Kid didn't reply, and he still hadn't spoken when they rode into Benson something like an hour later. They walked their horses down the main street and stopped in front of the marshal's office. A tall, thin man with a bushy mustache stepped through the open door and smiled at the old timer. The Kid saw the tin star on the man's chest and muttered another curse.

"Howdy, Jim!" the man said. "What brings you to town today?"

"Two things, Tom," the old timer said. He dismounted stiffly and stretched his back muscles. "First, I have a guest for you." Pulling the wanted poster from a vest pocket, the old timer unfolded it and handed it to the lawman. After reading it, the lawman looked up at the Kid.

"Step down, Kid Wilcox, and come on in," he said. "I'll show you to your room. Come on in out of the heat, Jim. I'll do a little paperwork and get your money for you."

"Make yourself comfortable, Kid," the lawman said. "It'll likely be a couple weeks before the circuit judge comes through again." He locked the door to the Kid's cell and turned to the old timer.

"What was the other thing that brought you to town today?" he asked.

"Shotgun shells," the old timer replied.

The lawman pulled several sheets of paper from a desk drawer and laid them on the desktop beside the Kid's poster. "Getting low on shells again?" he asked. With a stubby pencil he began to write.

"Not low," the old timer said. "I used my last shell on a jackrabbit a few days ago. I'm out."

The Kid had been sitting on the cot in his cell. He sprang to his feet, cursing, grabbed the bars with both hands, and rattled them. "What did you say?"

The old timer didn't reply. Grinning at the Kid, he broke open the shotgun to show the Kid two empty chambers. "I said I had an edge, Kid," he said. "I never said that my edge was this shotgun." He snapped the shotgun shut.

Again, the Kid rattled the door of his cell. Through gritted teeth he asked, "So, in spite of all your gabbing about it, you never really had an edge on me, did you?"

The old timer nodded his head slowly. "Oh, I had an edge, Kid," he said, "right from the beginning."

"What was it?" the Kid asked.

The old timer smiled. "I'm a whole lot smarter than you, Kid."

UNINVITED GUESTS

I am William Shakespeare Burton, fifteen years old and glad to be alive. My pa says I'm one of his top hands on our Arizona ranch, as hard-working as any full-grown man. Although hearing Pa say those things makes me feel like a man, I'm still fifteen. When my work is done, I want to play. Pa doesn't mind, and neither does Ma as long as she knows the general direction I'm headed when I saddle my horse.

Several months ago, while I was riding with my best friends, Clint and George Johnston, we discovered a deserted line shack in the northeast corner of their ranch, which lies just west of ours. We decided to make it our hideout. It was pretty run down, but we made it weatherproof. After stacking firewood and stocking the shelves with a few dry goods, we spent most of our free time there. We even stayed the night once.

Then as we rode up to the shack one afternoon, we found horses in our corral. We hid in the rocks until three men came out of the shack. Their guns were tied down, and the men were watchful, as if they were either expecting trouble or looking for it.

"Let's run them off," said George, starting toward the cabin.

"You lame brain!" Clint whispered, grabbing George's suspenders and pulling him back behind a rock. "They'll most likely shoot us. They're leaving anyway. Let's look around after they're gone."

The men saddled up and rode toward Peach Springs, six miles away. After they had disappeared over a ridge, we scrambled down the rock-covered slope to our shack.

The men planned to return. Two pack horses were still in the corral; and blanket rolls, saddlebags, and several boxes of ammunition were lying on the cot in the corner.

"Let's throw this stuff in the chaparral and bolt the door," said George.

"Let's not," I said.

"Look at this," Clint said. He handed a crumpled sheet of paper to George. The color left George's face as he read. Without speaking, handed the paper to me.

It was a "wanted" poster for the Willow Creek Gang. The reward was a thousand dollars for the leaders of the gang: Jack Hein, Frank Harris, and his brother Dave. There was no picture, but the description fit our visitors. They were wanted for robbery and murder.

"What are we going to do?" I whispered.

"I don't know," George replied. "Why are we whispering?"

After some discussion, we decided that Clint and George should ride to town and get Sheriff Parker while I kept an eye the shack from our hiding place in the rocks.

I watched them ride in the direction of town and then turned to look at the shack. Nothing looked out of place. The desperadoes would never suspect that we'd been there. Then I saw something that made me feel sick. A bright red piece of cloth was waving in the doorway. I felt my back pocket and found my gloves, but my bandanna was gone. I had been the last one through the door. When I had closed it behind me, I must have closed it on my bandanna.

If the men found it, they'd know that someone had been there. They'd get away before Clint and George could return with the sheriff.

I ran down to the shack, opened the door, and pulled out my bandanna. As I started back to my hiding place, a rock turned under my boot; and I fell, wrenching my ankle so hard that I yelled. I didn't know if I had broken it, but I quickly discovered that I couldn't walk on it.

I was sweating, but I felt a chill as I realized that the only place I could hide was inside the shack. With my ankle throbbing, I dragged myself back to the door and then inside. After closing the door, I scooted to the window that faced toward town and waited.

Gritting my teeth, I pulled off my boot. When I removed my sock, I saw that my ankle had swollen almost to the size of my knee. I groaned as I thought of how we had planned to spend our shares of the reward money. The money had looked like a sure thing, but now I reckoned there was a good chance that the outlaws would kill me and clear out before Clint and George returned with the sheriff.

As much as I hurt and as thirsty as I was, after a while I dozed. I awoke, confused, to the sound of hoof beats. Peeking out the corner of my window, I saw the riders starting down the slope toward the shack.

The only place to hide was barely big enough for me to squeeze my skinny carcass into, but I managed to scoot under the cot before the men entered. My ankle was throbbing, and I felt sick.

"How long do you reckon we'll be safe here, Frank?" one of the men asked.

"Just long enough to rest the horses," Frank replied.

"I'm so hungry I could—hey, Dave, did you hear somethin' out there?"

"You in the shack!" someone called from outside. "Shuck your guns and come out with your hands up. You're surrounded, so you can't escape."

One of the outlaws cursed. "How'd he know we was here? He must have spotted us in town, and now they've got us pinned down for sure!"

"What are we gonna do, Frank?" asked the man I reckoned was Dave.

"I'm not givin' myself over to no sheriff to get hung," Frank answered. "And if I go to hell, I'm not goin' alone." He drew his pistol and checked the cylinder. The man I thought was Jack sat on the cot with a box of bullets and began loading his rifle. In his haste he overturned the box, and two or three bullets rolled under the cot. Swearing, he got down on his hands and knees to pick them up. "We may need every bullet we can—what the— well, lookee here, boys!" He grabbed my arm and hauled me from my hiding place. "We got us a packrat!"

The one named Frank rubbed his whiskered chin and said, "No, we got us a hostage. What's your name, Boy?"

"B-Billy Burton, Sir," I said.

"Well, Billy Burton, I think you're about to do us a big favor." Frank went to the door, opened it a crack, and yelled, "Hey, Sheriff! We're comin' out, but we got someone with us by the name of Billy Burton. He might live to be an old man if you let us ride out of here. Give us a head start, and we'll send him back to you in the same shape we found him. What do ya' say?"

After a short pause, Sheriff Parker answered, "You have a deal; but if you hurt the boy, I'll hunt you down and see you hanged."

Frank pulled me off the cot where Dave had shoved me. He put his grizzled face close to mine.

"Listen, Kid," he said. "You behave yourself and you might see the sun rise tomorrow; but you try anything, and I'll blow your head off—understand?"

I nodded and said, "I c-can't walk, Sir. I think I b-broke my leg."

Frank swore under his breath. "Wouldn't you know it? Now what?"

The outlaw named Jack looked at me, I thought he was going to kill me right there. "Carry him, Dave," he said. "Frank and I will cover you."

"Why do I always have to—"

"Shut up, Dave," Frank said. "This ain't no time to argue. The kid can't be too heavy; and besides, you won't have to tote him for long."

When Dave picked me up, I yelled from the pain. He shook me. "Shut up, or I'll really hurt you, Kid!" he said.

I reckoned they were going to kill me if didn't do something soon. I was slung over Dave's shoulder like a feed sack. His arm rested across the back of my legs; and my face bounced off his dirty, sweat-soaked vest. After he had taken a dozen or more steps and was out in the open, I bit into his back as hard as I could. He yelled and cursed, but he also relaxed his grip. I slipped forward and thought I was going to hit the ground. Just then his arm tightened around my waist so that he had me in kind of a one-armed bear hug. I kneed him in the groin with my good leg. He screamed and fell to the ground. I screamed too—from fear and from pain—as I rolled over and over and slammed into a boulder.

I heard a dozen or more shots; then George and Clint were beside me, asking if I was hurt.

Jack and Frank had both been wounded. Dave had been captured easily because he had been unable to fight or run. On the way back to town, Sheriff Parker bragged pretty hard on us boys for the way we'd handled things.

Ma cried when I got home, but Pa said they were proud of us, too. Doc Billings said my ankle was only sprained; and in two weeks, I was as good as new. We had divided the reward money, which turned out to be fifteen hundred dollars instead of a thousand, three ways.

A month passed before we decided to visit our shack again. We were talking and laughing as we rode toward it. Suddenly, George stopped his horse and pointed.

"Look!" he said.

Four horses stood in the pole corral. We looked at each other for a minute. Then, without saying a thing, we turned our horses and raced toward town.

Look for the first book in the *Bounty Hunter* series, *Bounty Hunter Nate Landry: Major Issues*, by Mark L. Redmond, available at www.marklredmond.com and www.amazon.com for more western adventure. You can read the first chapter on the following pages.

The second book in the series, *Bounty Hunter Nate Landry: Family Fury*, is available at www.marklredmond.com and www.amazon.com as well.

BOUNTY HUNTER NATE LANDRY: MAJOR ISSUES

CHAPTER 1

If you ride north from Tucson in the general direction of Phoenix, you'll find a little town called Florence. If you ride west from Florence for another six miles, you'll cross a creek and find a cabin, snuggled against the butte. Whenever I say, "Honey, I'm home," I'm standing outside the door of that cabin. I live alone; but from time to time, someone else needs a dry spot for the night and spreads his blanket on the cabin floor. Since I don't fancy being shot, I like to warn people before I walk in on them. Besides, hearing those words as I come through the door always gives me a warm feeling—even when I know I'm only talking to myself.

I had been chasing a couple of desperadoes up near Phoenix. They weren't wanted for hanging offenses, so they had chosen going to the prison at Yuma over dying. I had delivered them to the town marshal in Phoenix and then waited in town until the bank in Prescott approved the reward. I had been away from my cabin for nearly a month when I pushed the door open and gave my familiar, friendly greeting. Startled wouldn't be a strong enough word for what I felt when I stepped into my cabin. This time "Honey" was home too.

She sat on one of the three chairs that are usually scooted up to the table that serves me for both eating and working. She had turned the chair to face the door; and since I was standing in the doorway, she was facing me. She was also pointing a gun at me.

"Don't move!" she said.

"I won't," I said.

While I was not moving, I studied the lady. She wore a pale blue shirt and a dark blue riding skirt. Her small, black boots reached almost to her knees; and the brim of a black hat, suspended from a cord around her neck, peeked over her shoulders from behind her. Her beautiful but expressionless face was sprinkled generously with freckles and surrounded by the brightest red hair I had ever seen. The revolver looked like an old .36 caliber Sheriff's model cap-and-ball, made in the South with some less expensive brass parts. The brass might not last as long as the steel parts used in the North, but this revolver looked to be clean and in working order. The .36 didn't have the stopping power of my .45, but it could easily kill me at this range.

"Could I move just enough to put my saddle down?" I asked.

"What makes you think you're staying?" she asked.

"I live here," I said. Slowly I lowered my saddle to the floor.

"I have only your word for that," she said. "Can you prove that this is your cabin?"

"Yes, Ma'am," I said, giving her my most charming smile. She basked in the charm for a full minute before she spoke.

"Well?" she asked, still basking.

"Well, what?" I asked, still smiling.

"Go ahead," she said.

"Why?" I asked. "I already know it's my cabin."

"Prove it to me," she said.

"Didn't you hear me say, 'Honey, I'm home'?" I asked.

She cocked the revolver, a strange action for one who was basking. "What kind of proof do you want?" I asked.

"Tell me where something is that only you know about," she said.

"You mean a secret?" I whispered. "Yes," she said.

"But we just met," I said. "I don't even know your name. I couldn't—"

Her .36 caliber ball splintered the floorboard between my feet. With a ringing in my ears and the smell of burned powder in my nostrils, I started over.

"Pleased to meet you, Ma'am," I said. "I have a scar on my back, high on my left shoulder. It's from when I got shot when I was just a boy. My brother Amos and I were—"

"A secret about this cabin," she said. "Tell me where something is hidden that only the owner would know about."

"Oh, I see," I said. "You mean something like the Remington .41 caliber derringer strapped to the bottom of your chair."

Gracefully she rose from the chair and then knelt beside it. I noticed that as she groped the bottom of the chair with her left hand, she kept her pale green eyes and her gun trained on me. I was impressed, especially since she was able to perform these tasks while still basking in my smile. She retrieved the gun from its hiding place and glanced at it.

"My name is Anna Thomas, Mr. Landry," she said. "I apologize for spoiling your home coming." She lowered her revolver, slid the derringer back into the leather strap, and stood beside the chair. "Please, come in. I have made some coffee, and I want to talk to you. I need your help."

"Obliged," I said. I poured each of us a cup of steaming coffee. "You haven't spoiled my home coming; and from what I've seen of you so far, Ma'am, if you need my help or anyone else's, you must have a very serious problem."

"I do," she said. She took a sip of coffee and then set her cup on the table. "My seven-year-old son was kidnapped from our ranch near Phoenix. The people who took him want $5000, delivered to the last relay station before Tucson on the road from Phoenix. The money is to be delivered Sunday at noon—that's only three days. If the money isn't delivered, or if anyone attempts to rescue him—" she stared into her cup.

"The boy dies," I said. "Do you have the money?"

"Yes," she said. "Virgil Hampton, who owns the bank, is—was one of David's close friends. He gave me—loaned me the five thousand dollars."

"What do you want from me?" I asked.

"I want you to bring back my son, unharmed—"

"Excuse the interruption, Ma'am," I said. "I know you came a long way to find me. I don't know how many days you've been waiting here for me—"

"Four," she said. "If you hadn't shown by tomorrow, I'd have gone alone."

"But," I said, "I'm not the man you want for delivering a ransom. I'm a—"

"I know what you are, Mr. Landry," she said. "I wasn't finished. After you have safely returned my son, I want you to hunt these men down and either kill them or bring them in to be hanged."

"Ma'am," I said, "I reckon that you must be afraid, worried, and angry; but I don't think there's a judge in the territory who would hang a man for stealing a kid as long as no harm came to—"

"My husband tried to stop the men who took Daniel, and they shot him down. He died the next day." Her green eyes were looking through me rather than at me. I saw hurt in them, but I saw determination as well.

"There are lawmen and other bounty hunters closer to your ranch," I said. "Why pick me?"

"I didn't," she said. "My husband's last words were, 'Find Nate Landry.'"

"What was your husband's first name?" I asked.

"David," she said.

I don't have the best memory in the world, but I reckoned I should be able to remember something about a man who had died with my name on his lips. I couldn't find even a ghost of a memory connected to that name. I looked again into those green eyes to see if they were hiding a lie. If there was one there, I couldn't find it. Still, something just didn't feel right. I had learned over the years to trust my gut feeling. I knew then that I was going to turn her down, but I thought it wouldn't hurt to ask one or two more questions.

"Do you have any idea who took the boy?" I asked.

"There were three of them," she said.

"Can you describe them and tell me what happened?" I asked.

She waited while I refilled my cup. "They must have been watching the ranch for a few days because they rode in about an hour after our ranch hands had left for the day," she said. "Usually at least one of them was still around somewhere, but that day we were there alone. David and Daniel were at the corral. Daniel was watching his father teach some of the green-broke horses to neck rein. I was watching from a window because some of those horses still have a lot of bucking left in them, and I was afraid David might get hurt." She sipped some coffee and then continued. "They rode from behind the house just after Dave had forked a new horse. He was so busy that I don't think he even saw them until one of them had grabbed Daniel from the top rail, swung him into the saddle in front of him, and started off at a gallop. When David saw what was happening, he threw himself from the saddle and ran to the corral fence, where he had hung his six-gun. About the time he got it clear of the holster, the other two started shooting. He never had a chance." She wiped her eyes with one hand.

"What did you do?" I asked.

"I grabbed David's rifle and ran onto the porch," she said. I emptied it at the two who had shot David. I think I might have hit the big one with the eye patch, but they still got away."

I felt a knot in the pit of my stomach. After the war, many soldiers in both gray and blue uniforms had returned to their homes with only one hand, one leg, one ear, or one eye. Certainly, many of the men who had lost an eye were big men. But how many of those one-eyed big men would steal a boy, kill his father, and then demand a ransom from his newly widowed mother? Not many would stoop that low, but I knew one who would. If that man had Daniel, the boy was in deep trouble.

As sorry as I was for this woman, her trouble was not my concern. I knew that my decision to turn her down was the right one. She could get help from the Pinkertons—maybe Allan Pinkerton himself. There were also two or three other reliable bounty hunters in the territory and several tough lawmen who would be able to help her. I just couldn't shake this bad feeling I had in my gut. I looked her in the eye, took a deep breath, and braced myself. Before I had a chance to speak, she stood, looking like a prisoner about to receive a death sentence.

"Will you help me, Mr. Landry?" she asked. "Yes, Mrs. Thomas, I will," I said.

"Thank you," she said. "I'll get some supper ready. We can get a good night's sleep and be on our way at first light."

Suddenly that bad feeling in my gut got worse.

Thank you for reading this book. I hope you found it both interesting and enjoyable. Please take a few minutes to leave a review on Amazon.com, Goodreads, BookBub, Facebook, or Instagram.

You can also leave a comment or ask a question at www.marklredmond.com or email me at markredmond53@gmail.com. Photos of you holding a copy of one of my books are always welcome.

Check the next page for a list of all my books. If you visit my website and join my posse, I'll email you updates on new books as they're published; and I'll and share other things that are happening in my world. My posse is growing, but there's room for you!

Books by Mark L. Redmond

The Arty Anderson Series
Arty Goes West
Arty and the Hunt for Phantom
Arty and the Texas Ranger
Arty's Long Day
Arty and the Cattle Rustlers
Arty's Tough Trail

The Nate Landry Series
Bounty Hunter Nate Landry: Major Issues
Bounty Hunter Nate Landry: Family Fury

The Box M Gang Series
The Box M Gang

Short Story Collections
Five for the Trail